Written by Quentin Flynn
Illustrated by Fifi Colston

Contents | Page

Nelson
an International Thomson Publishing company ITP®

The Great Egg Problem

With these characters ...

Guiseppe Bocconcini

Artemo Ricotta

Giovanni Parmesan

Maria Formaggio

Giorgio Mascarpone

Alessandra Mozzarella

"The great egg transporting

Setting the scene ...

In the sleepy summer of 1852, the mayor of Arrivederci is worried. His village survives on money made by the sale of its eggs. Unfortunately for Arrivederci, the road to Bellissimo, where the eggs are sold, is too rough and every egg is smashed before it reaches the market. No money for the village means a better road cannot be built. It's a tricky situation. Could there be a better way to transport the eggs? A way that ensures the eggs are not smashed along the way?

competition had begun!"

Prologue

In the summer of 1852, the tiny village of Arrivederci lay baking in the hot Italian sun. Perched high on a cliff, overlooking the Mediterranean Sea, the main street of the village was bordered by a row of stone houses. The only signs of life in the afternoon were a couple of dogs, who lay snoozing on the warm stone steps of one of the houses.

Beyond the village, in a rocky field, two old cart-horses stood, half-asleep, beneath the shade of a hand-painted sign that said "Guiseppe's Carting". Far beneath the village, the sea lapped gently at the base of the cliff.

Behind faded wooden doors, the inhabitants of Arrivederci were lulled to sleep by the sound of the sea. Their curtains were drawn tightly, shutting out the heat and the light, so they could relax and enjoy their afternoon siesta.

Apart from the sea, the only sound was the occasional snap of a dog's jaws as it chased away a lazy fly. Even the hens, for which Arrivederci was famous, sat dozing in their coops, waiting for the afternoon to cool down. All seemed peaceful in the Italian summer heat.

But, in the summer of 1852, all was not well with the village of Arrivederci. The mayor of the town, Artemo Ricotta, kept waking from his siesta. He had something on his mind. The future of his village was in danger.

Chapter 1.

Clunk! The wheels on Guiseppe Bocconcini's old wooden cart thumped into another pothole, and Guiseppe groaned. His horses tripped and stumbled along the bone-breaking track. Guiseppe looked nervously back at the rickety cart.

His precious cargo was bouncing around terribly. Crash! The cart banged against a boulder.

"Careful, Pop!" called out his son from the back of the cart. "We're only halfway to Bellissimo, and already we've smashed half the cargo!"

Guiseppe tried to steer his horses along the bumpy, rocky road. He concentrated on the potholes in the road, and closed his eyes every time they hit one. Unfortunately, he knew that when he returned to his home village of Arrivederci, there would be some very angry people waiting for him.

"This road used to be in good condition. Now it's hardly a road at all!" he thought.

Slowly, a slimy yellow mixture started dribbling out of the back of the cart. With every crash and thump of the cart, the dribble turned into a steady stream.

"Careful!" yelled out the boy again.

Guiseppe couldn't do anything to be more careful. The winter rains had washed most of the soil away from the cart track, and all that was left were great, sharp-edged boulders, and huge, rough potholes.

When Guiseppe finally arrived at the seaside market town of Bellissimo, he could hardly bear to inspect the damage. His son had given up telling him to be careful, and that could only mean one thing. The cargo was ruined.

As he climbed down from his cart and walked around to the rear, Guiseppe saw a yellow trail along the road. Looking most distressed, his son wiped gooey yolk out of his eyes and hair.

"Oh, no," he whistled, as he and his son looked at the slimy mess.

Throughout the inside of Guiseppe's cart were thousands of broken egg shells, like a crazy mosaic. Not one egg was left intact.

"We have to solve this problem," said Guiseppe, shaking his head.

Chapter 2.

Arrivederci was famous all over Italy for the eggs that its hens laid—lovely, tasty eggs, with yolks the colour of a warm sunset. Eggs that could be made into the most delicious cakes, desserts and pasta! Arrivederci's eggs provided all the villagers with enough money to live a comfortable life.

From Bellissimo, sailing ships would take Arrivederci's famous eggs to towns and cities up and down Italy's west coast. The villagers' problem was that the ten kilometres of rocky road that linked Arrivederci with Bellissimo was quickly getting rougher.

On each trip, no matter how careful Guiseppe tried to be, most of the eggs were smashed.

Nobody at the market in Bellissimo wanted to buy scrambled eggs. The villagers were running out of money.

With no income from the eggs, the villagers could not afford to repair their road. The village council also had very little money. But Mayor Artemo Ricotta dreamed up a plan that afternoon, during his siesta—one that might just save the tiny village of Arrivederci from poverty.

Artemo Ricotta heard Guiseppe's cart rumbling back into town. As he looked out his window, he saw a crowd of villagers had gathered around the cart. Everyone was arguing noisily and waving their arms about furiously.

Artemo rolled himself out of bed, and carefully put on his black top hat. He puffed out his chest and did up the top button of his pyjamas. At his writing desk, he picked up his quill, dabbed it in ink, and began to write "The Official Arrivederci Proclamation".

As the summer sun turned the sky the colour of a glorious egg yolk, the villagers sat around in the town square grumbling and blaming Guiseppe for smashing their eggs yet again. They watched curiously as Artemo Ricotta strode from his house towards the town's noticeboard. Their mayor was looking very important in his black top hat. What was going on?

He pinned a large notice on the noticeboard and, with a very official-looking nod of his head, surveyed his work. The more curious villagers came closer, and peered over his shoulder to read the notice.

The Official Arrivederci Proclamation!

I, Artemo Ricotta, Mayor of the fine village of Arrivederci, do solemnly proclaim a competition shall be held. The competition shall be known as the Great Egg Transporting Competition. The grand judging of the competition will be held in the town square in one month's time. The designer of the best method or device by which the precious eggs of this village can be safely transported to Bellissimo shall receive a prize of one thousand lira.

By authority of the Mayor

on this first day of June, 1852.

Artemo Ricotta.

One thousand lira! The villagers looked at each other. One thousand lira was a fortune! All the villagers were keen to think up a design. There could be no more siestas in the afternoon! There was no time to lose. There were plans to be drawn up; models to be made; designs to be tested. The Great Egg Transporting Competition had begun!

During the next few weeks, the village of Arrivederci looked the same from the outside. In the afternoons, the dogs still lay snoozing on the warm stone steps. Guiseppe's ancient cart-horses still stood in the shade of his sign. Far beneath the village, the sea still lapped gently at the base of the cliff. But there were different sounds in the village.

Behind the faded wooden doors, the villagers of Arrivederci were working hard. Their curtains were drawn tightly, not to shut out the heat and the light, but to keep their plans, models and designs secret until the very last minute.

Guiseppe no longer had any eggs to transport to Bellissimo. Everyone was keeping their eggs for a much more important purpose. Inside houses all over the village, eggs were dropped, smashed, bumped, broken and splattered as people tested their designs.

Every evening, people would appear from their houses, their hair streaked with egg yolks, and their faces covered in bits of egg and egg shell. But no-one breathed a word to anyone from another family. A thousand lira was too much money to risk spies learning about their inventions.

With only a day to go before the judging, everyone was making final adjustments to their inventions. There was an air of mystery and excitement in the village. Who would win the thousand lira? Who would rescue the fortunes of Arrivederci and make it, once more, the egg capital of Italy?

On the day of the competition, Artemo Ricotta buttoned up his finest white shirt, pulled on his most official-looking pair of braces, and dusted off his top hat. He admired himself in the mirror, and practised looking official. He was about to judge the competition that would save the village.

Chapter 3.

Outside, in the town square, a crowd was gathering.

The Parmesan family, led by Giovanni Parmesan, stood behind a large object wrapped in brown paper and string.

The Formaggio family, led by Maria Formaggio, stood behind a dome-shaped package, covered by a blanket.

The Mascarpone family, led by Giorgio Mascarpone, stood proudly behind a cardboard box, placed on a small table.

The Mozzarella family, led by Alessandra Mozzarella, stood with their arms folded, a big sack at their feet.

The only person who was not there was Guiseppe Bocconcini, the man who owned the cart-horses.

Mayor Artemo Ricotta strode into the middle of the street and raised his arms in a very official manner. The crowd fell silent, and all that could be heard was the distant sound of the waves gently washing up against the cliff below.

"Today, as mayor of the fine village of Arrivederci, I have the solemn and serious task of judging a competition, the very competition that was initiated one month ago. That was initiated by me," he added, in case anyone was in any doubt about how important he really was.

"I declare that the judging shall commence."

With a grand gesture (that he had been practising all morning), Artemo pointed at the large object, wrapped in brown paper and string, in front of the Parmesan family.

Giovanni Parmesan stepped forward, untied the knots in the string and removed the paper. The crowd murmured. In front of them stood a large wooden bucket, filled with water. In the water, several eggs were floating.

“We shall place this on the back of Guiseppe’s cart,” explained Giovanni Parmesan. “The water will cushion the floating eggs as the cart bumps over the rocky track.” He beamed and looked around. The crowd nodded in unison.

"Very well," said Artemo, who was impressed. With another grand gesture, he pointed to the dome-shaped package, covered by a blanket, in front of the Formaggio family. Maria Formaggio, with a flourish, pulled off the blanket. The crowd murmured again.

Under the blanket was a perfectly round balloon, made of thin paper, glued in strips. At the bottom was an opening and a tiny candle, attached by string. Maria lit the candle and, to the crowd's astonishment, the paper balloon filled with hot air and lifted off the ground.

“We shall tie an egg under each balloon,” explained Maria Formaggio, “and then attach all the balloons to Guiseppe’s cart-horses. The eggs will fly all the way to Bellissimo,” she said. She bowed, and the crowd burst into applause.

"Very well," said Artemo, who was impressed. He turned to the Mascarpone family, and grandly gestured in the direction of their cardboard box. Giorgio Mascarpone carefully unfolded the lid of the box, and drew out a large square of fishing net, with ropes attached to each corner.

"Two corners of the net are tied to each of Guiseppe's horses," explained Giorgio. "The eggs are carefully placed in each hole in the net, and the horses walk beside each other, all the way to Bellissimo, with the net between them. The eggs will gently sway over all the bumps!" Giorgio grinned at the crowd, who were clapping again. Someone even called out "Bravo!"

Artemo was most impressed but, of course, it would be very unofficial to show it. He kept a stern face, and waved at the Mozzarella family's sack. Alessandra Mozzarella unfolded her arms and untied the string around the sack's neck.

A sudden gust of wind filled the air with feathers, swirling out of the sack. Artemo, who was peering into the sack at the same time, struggled to brush the tiny white feathers off his top hat, his shirt and his moustache. It would not do for the mayor to look completely ridiculous on such an important day!

"I'm very sorry," said Alessandra Mozzarella. "My design has been cleverly adapted from nature," she continued. "What is the safest place for an egg before it is laid?"

Everyone looked puzzled. Artemo pretended he knew, even though he had no idea what Alessandra was talking about.

"Inside a hen, of course!" said Alessandra. Artemo nodded wisely.

"So we should put all our eggs in hen-sized sacks full of feathers before we put them on Guiseppe's cart. That way, they will stay unbroken on the rocky road."

Artemo nodded again.

Finally, he scratched his chin and looked thoughtful. They all seemed like excellent designs. Who was he going to give the prize to?

Just when Artemo was about to announce a winner, someone shouted, "Wait!"

Chapter 4.

"Here comes Guiseppe!" shouted Mrs Bocconcini. "He's got something under his arm."

Artemo was about to protest that the entries had closed, but the crowd turned to look at Guiseppe. He was strolling down the rocky field towards the village, with something rolled up under his arm. As he got closer, everyone could see it was a long, coiled piece of strong rope.

"Here is my entry," smiled Guiseppe, as he walked into the middle of the crowd and dropped his coil of rope on the ground.

"I believe the thousand lira prize will be mine!"

Everyone looked bewildered.

"Er, perhaps you might explain your entry first?" said Artemo, who was confused.

"That road is too bumpy to transport a cart full of eggs. I will use my thousand lira to build my horses a nice, shady stable and to buy them bales of thick, golden hay. They have been good horses, and they need a rest."

"But how will you get your cart to Bellissimo?" asked Artemo, even more confused. "All these inventions rely on your horses and your cart."

"I don't have my cart anymore," smiled Guiseppe. "This morning in Bellissimo, I swapped it for something more useful."

The villagers couldn't believe their ears. Now, they would *never* be able to get their eggs to market!

"Are you mad?" spluttered Artemo. "What about our eggs? How will we get them to Bellissimo?"

"With the help of this," replied Guiseppe, pointing to the rope. "And with the help of *Maria Rosa*," he said, folding his arms and grinning.

"Who?" asked Artemo in exasperation.

Guiseppe beckoned. The villagers followed him as he walked down the main road to the cliff. They cautiously peered over and saw a rope ladder. It led down to a small red sailing boat, gently bobbing at anchor below.

"All you have to do is lower baskets full of eggs, tied to this long rope, to me in the *Maria Rosa*," explained Guiseppe. "With a good wind, it only takes me an hour to sail to Bellissimo. No rocks. No potholes. No stumbling horses. No bumps. And best of all—*no* broken eggs."

The villagers looked amazed. What a simple answer! Why hadn't anyone thought of that before?

Artemo drew himself up into his most official-looking posture, and took off his top hat.

"We have a winner," he said in a very grand tone, shaking Guiseppe's hand vigorously. The crowd clapped and cheered, and even the Parmesans, Formaggios, Mascarpones and Mozzarellas smiled and nodded their heads.

Artemo handed over the thousand lira to Guiseppe, and the crowd applauded enthusiastically. The village was saved! Everyone was in high spirits, talking and planning what they would do with the extra money that the sale of the eggs would bring.

Artemo stood watching the happy villagers.

"You know, Artemo," he said to himself. "Every problem can be solved. But it takes the cleverest minds to see the simplest solution."

"Just like my own clever mind. I think I'll hold competitions for all our village problems in future. It will save me having to think up my own solutions!"

Artemo chuckled most unofficially, and closed the faded door of his house behind him. It was time for a siesta. Outside, the villagers danced and sang until the sun went down and the moon came up over Arrivederci. A full round moon, like a gigantic egg in the sky.

"The future of his village was in danger!"

To Bellissimo, eggs must go!
But the road, damaged and slow,
Leaves eggs splattered and smashed,
And a village short of cash.

Eggs could fly, eggs could float,
Go by horse, or go by boat!
Either way, they must be sent;
What method of transport
Would *you* invent?